Sara Henderson Smith

**Up to the Light with Other Religious and Devotional Poems**

Sara Henderson Smith

**Up to the Light with Other Religious and Devotional Poems**

ISBN/EAN: 9783337270575

Printed in Europe, USA, Canada, Australia, Japan

Cover: Foto ©Andreas Hilbeck / pixelio.de

More available books at **www.hansebooks.com**

WITH OTHER

# RELIGIOUS AND DEVOTIONAL POEMS.

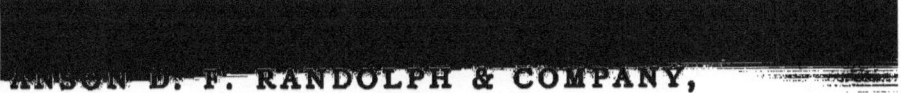

ANSON D. F. RANDOLPH & COMPANY,

900 BROADWAY, COR. 20th STREET.

EDWARD O. JENKINS' SONS,
*Printers and Stereotypers*,
North William St., New York.

# PREFACE.

Sara Henderson Smith, the author of the Poems embraced in the accompanying selection, was the daughter of Dr. Thomas Henderson, late of the U. S. Army, and the wife of General Francis H. Smith, of the Virginia Military Institute. Her mother was a daughter of the late Commodore Thomas Truxtun, U. S. Navy.

In a private memorandum found among her papers, there is the following record :

### OLD AGE IN DEATH.

#### BY E. WALLER.

The seas are quiet, when the winds give o'er,
So calm are we when passions are no more.
For then we know how vain it was to boast,
Of fleeting things, too certain to be lost.
Clouds of affection from our younger eyes
Conceal that emptiness which age descries.

The soul's dark cottage, shattered and decayed,
Lets in new light, through chinks that time has made.
Stronger by weakness, wiser, men become,

(3)

As they draw near to their eternal home ;
Leaving the old, both worlds, at once, they view,
That stand upon the threshold of the new.

"The first two lines of the second stanza were among the last words distinctly uttered by my grandmother, SARA, widow of ALEXANDER HENDERSON, of Dumfries, Prince William County, Virginia.

"My grandmother was remarkable for intellectual gifts, which throughout her life she continued to cultivate by extensive reading, and every means afforded in her day. To a poetical temperament, she added a love of music, and a voice of great power and sweetness. Her four daughters were carefully instructed in music—all of them good musicians; two were very distinguished ; my father, the only one of her sons who inherited this gift. I have heard him say when other opportunity was not afforded, his mother tuned her own piano. A married life, more than ordinarily blessed, and continuing nearly half a century, was followed by one year of widowhood."

The "intellectual gifts," as well as the name of her grandmother, were the rich heritage of SARA HENDERSON SMITH, and it is believed the accompanying selection from her Devotional Poems will fully illustrate and confirm the gift of Poesy.

This little volume will be followed by another, containing some of her brightest miscellaneous pieces, many of which were written in her earlier years.

Like her grandmother, "her married life was more than ordinarily blessed, and continuing nearly half a century," closed at the Virginia Military Institute, Lexington, Va., May 18, 1884.

VIRGINIA MILITARY INSTITUTE,
*June* 9, 1884.

# CONTENTS.

B E this my token when I am gone!
   The child, to remember a pleasant word;
The servant, a burden laid lightly on;
   The desolate waif, a feeling stirred
Kindlier far than when she came
For the trifle offered in His dear Name.

Be this my token when I am gone!
   The hand that could give, but not withhold;
Prouder than record on sculptured stone,
   Richer than treasures of burnished gold;
The tongue that could bless, but never defame,
Patient, enduring, for His dear Name.

Rough though the pathway our footsteps tread,
   Hedged with thorns lest we turn aside—
He, the Sinless, oft laid His head
   On the cold mountains at eventide.
The brow that had worn a kingly crown,
With the night-dews heavy—with grief bowed
      down.

Be this my token when I am gone!
   Dimly reflecting His heart of love,
Tears dried from eyes that had still wept on,
   Dimming with shadows the light above.
And love, and service, and life complete,
May the servant rest at the dear Lord's feet.

S. H. S.

# UP TO THE LIGHT,

## AND OTHER POEMS.

---

### UP TO THE LIGHT.

" UP to the light," said the blade of grass,
    " The clods are heavy, and I must pass
Patiently—gropingly on my way,
Till I pierce the darkness and find the day.
What though an atom in time and space—
Even an atom may claim its place;
And, toiling upward, I fulfil
All that I know of my Master's will."

" Up to the light," said the tiny bird,
    As dawn the depths of the forest stirred,
    And a joyful song rang out afar
    Clear and bright as the morning star.
" What though an atom in time and space—
    Even an atom may claim its place;
    And singing heavenward, I fulfil
    All that I know of my Master's will."

" Up to the light," said the struggling soul,
" The twilight deepens—the shadows roll
    Fitfully, fearfully, over my head,
    And the spirit within me is cold and dead.

Every atom in time and space
Claims for itself its destined place—
While I, a cumberer, through my days
Faint in labor, and fail in praise."

"'Up to the light,' their way must lie—
They are willing workers—but what am I ?
Wasting the wealth of priceless hours
On fleeting triumphs and fading flowers;
No more a dreamer in time and space,
Lord, of Thy goodness, appoint my place,
That loving, and serving I may fulfil
All that I know of my Master's will."

"'Up to the light,' through doubts and fears—
Up through the mists of many tears—
Up the steep ascent whose summits rise
Till lost in the blue of the upper skies;
There, in the realms of Eternal day,
Sorrow and sighing shall flee away,
Rough or lonely the path may be,
Upward, still upward, it leads to Thee."

*SAY THE SWEET WORDS AGAIN.*

" Wherefore He is able also to save them to the uttermost that
come unto God by Him."—Heb. vii. 25.

SAY the sweet words again—
    Are they for me?

" Save to the uttermost,"
   Lord, can it be !
I, once the chief of all,
Slighting Thy mercy's call,
Fast bound in Satan's thrall,
   Can I be free ?

Sin, with its iron chain
   Fetters me still ;
Evil I would not do,
   Conquers my will.
Oh ! for the liberty
Wherewith Christ makes us free ;
Lord, most complete in me,
   Thy work fulfil.

As some poor castaway,
   Nearing the shore,
Grasping a friendly hand,
   Fears death no more ;
So while the waves run high,
Strong in Thy strength—may I
On Thy great love rely,
   All doubting o'er.

Thou hast said, " It is I,
   Be not afraid,
My perfect work is done,
   Thy ransom paid."

Only for Him who died,
Jesus, the Crucified,
Be all my sin and pride
    At His feet laid.

Loud Hallelujahs ring
    Through the high heaven ;
Peace, with the starlit morn
    Is to earth given.
Now, then, my soul, be strong—
Take up the Angel's Song—
And while it floats along,
    Be thy bonds riven.

*Christmas Eve.*

## I AM WANDERING, I AM WANDERING.

" Jesus said, If thou knewest the gift of God, thou wouldest
have asked of Him, and He would have given thee living water."
" Whosoever drinketh of this water (of earth) shall thirst again."
" But whosoever drinketh of the water that I shall give him,
shall never thirst."—JOHN iv. 10, 13.

" I AM wandering, I am wandering,
    In this weary world alone ;
I have proved all earthly pleasures,—
    I am satisfied in none.

" Half real—half unreal—
    A higher life than this,

Floats before my mental vision—
  Can you tell me what it is?

" For this my soul is longing,
    Yet I may not bid it stay;
  Ere I grasp the bright illusion,
    It has fluttered far away!"


" It is written "—read the record—
    The characters are plain;
" They who drink from earthly fountains,
    Shall surely thirst again."

" But the cup that I will give thee,
    So free to all—so pure,—
  I have filled with living waters,—
    He who drinks, shall thirst no more."


" My Saviour, hast Thou offered
    Eternal life to me?
  Bought by Thy precious bloodshed—
    Thy bitter agony!

" Come, then, and take possession
    Of all that is Thy own;
  For the immortal spirit
    Finds rest in Thee alone."

2

## ADMONITION.

"What I say unto you, I say unto all, Watch."—MARK xiii. 37.

ONE, from your ranks, has fallen away,
    Worthily wearing your garb of grey;
One vacant seat at your mess-hall board—
One well-known name from your class roll
    scored—
One youthful form, in the spring-time's birth,
Sadly borne to its native earth.

Summer dies with its laughing bloom—
Life, in the glad new year shall come,
Dancing waters lie still in death—
Life springs up with the south wind's breath,
But the body and spirit of man, in twain,
Never on earth shall be one again.

Gone from our sight, to that far-off bourne,
Whence the steps of the traveller never return,
No sound comes back to the waiting ear;—
Nought for our lost but the pall—the bier—
And words falling heavily—fall, they must—
"Ashes to ashes"—"dust to dust."

Can all of our being be bound within
This narrow circle of death and sin?
Can the soul the Glorified came to save,
Die with the treasure we give the grave?

Better by far that earthly love
Never its sheltering tendrils wove.


Look up—look up—through the darkened night,
Thanks be to God, He giveth light.
Look up—look up—to Him who saith
" Fear not—*I* have the keys of death ! "
At the shadowy portal angels wait—
Look to the Life beyond the gate.

———

Jesus, at your conscience knocking,
    Whispers, " Frail as he, thou art."
Satan still, without, is blocking
    Every pathway to your heart.
Shall your Lord neglected wait,
Till you pass the shadowy gate !


While that heart's warm tears are gushing
    Heed, oh ! heed the warning sound ;
Lest your footsteps still be rushing
    On uncertain, slippery ground,
Till you reach the shadowy gate ;—
Lest for *you*, no angels wait.


He the Life—the Resurrection—
    He who holds your fleeting breath,
Only asks the soul's affection,—
    Pleads to rescue you from death.

Will you linger—will you wait—
Till you reach the shadowy gate?

"They that seek" Him "early"—"find Him."
  Freshest from the new-born day,
Flowers of hope and promise bind Him.
  Bearing still His Cross alway,
Till you leave it at the gate,
Where with crowns the angels wait.

-------

## *YOU HAVE GIRDED ON YOUR ARMOR.*

"Thou therefore be strong."   "Endure hardness as a good soldier of Jesus Christ."—2 TIM. ii. 1-3.

YOU have girded on your armor,
  You have rallied side by side;
Naught upon your stainless banner,
  Save a cross, all crimson-dyed;
Nothing, save the blessed token
  Of a bleeding Saviour's love;
Once on earth a Man of Sorrows—
  Now a Prince enthroned above.

May your way be onward, upward,
  Though your feet oft travel-worn;
May the wounded, fainting spirit,
  Never whisper of return:

Though the soul-betraying tempter
  Bid the Christian warfare cease,
May you onward press and upward—
  So He gives His people peace.

There are well-springs in the desert,
  Where the lone and weary rest—
There's a Friend whose arm is stronger
  Than the foe within your breast:
Ever near your glorious Leader
  You cannot suffer loss;
For earth has no such triumphs,
  As the triumphs of the Cross.

In the flush of early manhood
  Some may lay their armor down;
Some, in the sultry noontide,
  May win the victor's crown:
Some, toiling on till evening,
  Find rest at close of day;—
But from every brow the burden
  Of the strife is wiped away.

Beyond the purple rim of morning,
  Bathed in floods of living light,
Gleams "Jerusalem the Golden"
  With its towers and banners bright:
Then onward still, and upward,
  In the path that Jesus trod,

Who bore our sins to lead us
To the City of our God.

V. M. Institute, *May 16th,* 1869.

Confirmation by Bishop Whittle.   Forty-eight cadets confirmed
and admitted to membership with the Church of Christ on earth.

" Thanks be unto God for His unspeakable gift."

---

## *" WE LOVE HIM BECAUSE HE FIRST LOVED US."*—1 John iv. 19.

I HEARD a voice—the gentlest tone
  That ever fell on mortal ear ;
It might have touched a heart of stone,
  Alas ! a harder heart was here.
It said that " pleasure, fame and power
  In youthful dreams were fair to see ";
' But they are phantoms of an hour—
  I am eternal.   FOLLOW ME ! "

In vain He plead.   I see Him now
  So patient with my rash disdain ;
Turning with careless lip and brow
  From Him, my Lord, oft and again.
In Satan's iron fetters bound,
  What could disturb my fancied peace ?
" The world is fair," I said, " when found
  No more to charm, Thy words may please."

He spoke of wealth.   The proud, rich man
  Who laid him down self-satisfied,
Then started—thus the summons ran :
  " Thou fool—this night!" and   heard, and
         died !
Of one who sat upon a throne,
  And while the people worshipped, fell,
Eaten of worms and stricken down,
  Forever with the lost to dwell.

In vain He plead !  He told of him
  For whom all pleasure's gifts came free ;
Whose cup was sparkling to the brim,
  Who drank and called it " Vanity ! "
In vain ! my heart more stubborn grew,
  Rebellion struggled fierce within ;
From pride of intellect I drew
  Food for my folly and my sin.

Once more He came.   Asked would I learn
  Of all His love had borne for me ;
Spoke of His wounds, His crown of thorns,
  His soul's dark hour of agony.
That look of love,—at last it swept
  The barriers of my sin away ;
And when I thought thereon, I wept,
  And at His feet repentant lay.

That look of love, for sinners sealed
  In anguish on the blood-stained Cross,

My guilt and helplessness revealed ;
   And now I count all gain but loss
For the dear honor of His name.
   Lord, let it still abide with me,
Lest I forget in wealth or fame,
   The ransom paid on Calvary.

---

## HE IS CALLING MANY ROUND ME.

" Hear what comfortable words our Saviour Christ saith unto all
who truly turn to Him: 'Come unto me, all ye that labor and are
heavy laden, and I will give you rest.' "—St. MATT. xi. 28.

H E is calling many round me,
   And they say His voice is sweet,
That they can not choose but follow,
   And worship at His feet :
That the hardest heart is melted
   By love so great, so free,
But to me He has not spoken,—
   No message comes to *me.*

It is a day of mercy,
   Will He not hear my cry?
He came to ransom sinners,
   And will He pass me by?
No other hand can save me,
   Can take away my sin ;

'Tis Thine, oh! precious Saviour,
   'Tis Thine, to wash me clean.

What if the world be given,
   What were an earthly crown,
If my soul from life eternal
   To death and hell go down?
No, it is *all*, or *nothing!*
   Then let my portion be,
No lingering and no doubting,
   My Saviour, near to Thee.

Oh! Love divine, exceeding!
   Thy voice is in my heart;
" Fear not, for I am with thee,
   Thine is the better part."
No more can earthly pleasures
   My senses steal away;
They fade as fades the darkness
   Before the light of day.

On earth the Cross is hallowed,—
   In Heaven the crown is won,
When the pearly gates are opened,
   And salvation's work is done.
*Here*, still my footsteps guiding,
   Thy love shall be my stay;
*There!* farewell, night and shadow,
   Welcome, eternal day!

## *MY SON, GIVE ME THY HEART.*

"GIVE me thy heart," while youth is wreath-
        ing
    Garlands of flowers to twine thy brow—
" Give me thy heart," while joy is breathing
    A spell of promise around thee now.

" Give me thy heart "—while every feeling
    Thrills to the spirit's rapturous play—
" Give me thy heart," ere age is stealing
    Its first, best energies away.

I ask no crown of jewelled splendor,
    No glittering treasure from the mine ;
I only ask the heart's surrender.
    Come, lay it at thy Father's shrine.

## *SONG OF THE DEEP SEA.*

OFT alone, not lonely,
    Must the spirit be ;
Where the ear can hear them,
    Where the eye can see,
Move the surface waters,
    Fretting, surging on,

While unbroken stillness
  Marks the depths unknown,
So the soul's rude turmoil
  Is for fellow-man;
But its hidden workings
  He may never scan.


Friends pause at the portal
  Veiled with anxious care;
One, our Elder Brother,
  Only enters there;
Sees our sore temptation,—
  Hears our pleading call,—
Pities, ere we speak them,
  For He knows them all.
Be the inner temple
  Then divinely pure;
Only hallowed footsteps
  Tread the sacred floor.


There we guard our treasures,—
  Tender words of love,
Free from earth's defilings
  As the stars above.
There we weep our sorrows,
  While the lip smiles on,
Glad that to the Master
  Is the servant known;

Patient for the token
   Swept along the sea,
" Fear thou not the trial,
   I have sent it thee."

Earth must have its guerdon—
   Days must come and go,
Like the upper waters
   In their ceaseless flow.
But the deep sea quiet
   Bears within its breast
Germs of higher teaching,
   Types of perfect rest;
Ever as the sea-shell
   Murmurs of the sea,
Bearing still a message,
   " Peace He giveth thee."

## *PRAYER.*

FATHER! I would this wayward heart
   Might on Thy promised love repose—
I would Thy Spirit might impart
   To mine, some balm for human woes.

The world which I have worshipped long
   Has failed me in the hour of grief—

Its fascinations, once so strong,
  Can never more afford relief.

Thou who hast said Thou ne'er will turn
  Heedlessly away from misery,
Thou! who hast promised ne'er to spurn
  The contrite heart that clings to Thee,

Oh! send me not unblest away—
  A suppliant at Thy throne I bow.
On Thee I fix the only ray
  Of hope that lingers round me now.

Give me a portion of Thy grace—
  Thy Love's rich treasure on me pour;
Show me the brightness of Thy face,
  And let me love the world no more.

---

## THE SECOND SUNDAY IN ADVENT.

" That we through patience and comfort of the Scriptures might
have hope."—Rom. xv. 4.

WE need to wait in patience—
    One who is gone before,
Had a weary life upon this earth,
  But all his sorrows o'er,
In glory and in majesty,
  He reigneth evermore.

We need to wait in patience—
  Affection's broken chain,
Our restless hearts with quenchless love,
  Would strive to link in vain ;
The lost one to the yearning breast,
  Returneth not again.

We need to wait in patience—
  From all defilement free—
To holy thoughts with purpose strong,
  As a sure refuge flee,
For as our Master knew no guile,
  Pure should His servants be.

We need to wait in patience—
  Our treasures are not here—
The Christian traveller murmurs not,
  Although the way be drear ;
His guide-book points no resting-place,
  Unless his Lord be near.

We need to wait in patience—
  Our Father wills it so ;
Nor idly wait—but day by day,
  With help and comfort go,
To wayworn, fellow-pilgrims
  In a world of toil and woe.

And we may wait in comfort—
  For still on angel wing,

Our shield from soul-destroying ease—
Our help in suffering—
His messengers from every foe
Shall swift deliverance bring.

In comfort and in hope,
His patient children wait ;
Oh ! with what tenderness He looks
Upon their low estate ;
And gently leads their wandering feet
To the Celestial Gate.

## THE UNSEALED FOUNTAIN.

" In that day there shall be a fountain opened for sin and for uncleanness."—ZECH. xiii. 1.

" HO every one that thirsteth "
Here living waters flow,
Come to the crystal fountain—
Come with your sin and woe—
No price—no ransom bringing—
Ye heavy-laden come—
For Christ the Lord is waiting—
He calls His ransomed home.

O'er many a snow-capped mountain,
On many a waving plain—

A voice of love is telling
  Of One for sinners slain.
The red man on his war-path
  No more shall blindly roam ;
For Christ the Lord is waiting—
  He calls His ransomed home.

From Afric's burning deserts
  Her dusky sons we meet ;
Brought out for toil and travail—
  Led on with captive feet ;
They hear the Gospel message
  Across the wild waves foam :
For Christ the Lord is waiting—
  He calls His ransomed home.

Our fathers, sons, and brothers,
  The subtle tempter's prey,
Here quench the restless fires
  That waste your souls away.
Your sins, though red like crimson,
  Shall white as snow become ;
For Christ the Lord is waiting—
  He calls His ransomed home.

Look on the Cross uplifted !
  Who would this Love repay ;
Go, seek the lost—the erring—
  Once you were blind as they ;

Go, tell the "old, old story"
  Till countless throngs shall come ;—
For Christ the Lord is waiting—
  He calls His ransomed home.

----

## THE FIRST SUNDAY IN ADVENT.

" The night is far spent ; the day is at hand."—ROM. xiii. 12.

NOW the rosy morn is breaking
  O'er the long benighted earth,
Prophets' stars have held their waking,
  Till the glorious sun beamed forth ;
Youth and maiden rise to meet Him,
  Hoary head and infant fair,
With loud hallelujahs greet Him,
  Let hosannas fill the air.

See ye Him in royal splendor,
  With a lordly, glittering train,
Bidding kings their pomp surrender,
  Through His peerless, wide domain ?
No ; He cometh meek and lowly,
  With Salvation's garments clad,
Bow in reverence, He is holy,
  Praise with joy, He maketh glad.

Man's proud heart is His dominion,
　　There His sceptre holds its sway,
Peace and Love, on angel pinion,
　　Saviour-King, attend Thy way ;
Guilt, with doubt and fear oppressing,
　　He can break thy captive thrall,
With unerring wisdom blessing,
　　Princely gifts He offers all.


Souls, redeemed from sin and sorrow,
　　Gird the heavenly armor on,
Victory waits the coming morrow,
　　Conflict with the night is gone ;
Slumber not, the foe is waking—
　　Pause not, He is ever near—
Onward, till the morn is breaking,
　　Rest was never promised here.


Once again thy Lord descending,
　　On Mount Olivet shall stand,
Ransomed hosts are round Him bending,
　　O'er Him waits an angel band ;
Then, throughout the wide creation,
　　Let your shout of triumph ring—
Morning breaks, with adoration,
　　Victors ! greet your Saviour-King.

## THE FOURTH SUNDAY IN ADVENT.

"Rejoice in the Lord alway." "The Lord is at hand."—
PHIL. iv.

WHO that awaits a father dear,
When he our distant path would cheer,
But knows that for the honored guest,
With every charm the home is drest,
And feels how light the labors prove,
That follow in the steps of love !

The room arranged with anxious care—
The softened light that is not gloom—
The well-known books—the favorite chair—
Some tokens of our early home
Long treasured—now brought out to speak
Of ties that absence can not break.

Our task complete—how oft reviewed—
Still deem we some thing left undone ;
And strive to catch in thoughtful mood,
Some fancy of the cherished one ;
Nor pause, till in his fond embrace,
The heart has found its resting-place.

. . . . . . . . .

Thou, more than father—more than friend—
How should our spirits watch for Thee,
Who, with transcending love, didst bend
To guard our helpless infancy,

Our erring, wayward youth—and still
Our life doth shield from every ill.

No more, indeed, an infant fair,
    We lay our treasures at Thy feet,—
No more our blest abode to share,
    With joy Thy hallowed form we greet,
No more we soothe Thy weariness,
Nor worship where Thy footsteps press.

And yet, oh ! Blessed One, Thou art
    To every true Disciple near ;
Still may each faithful, trusting heart,
    Expectant wait till Thou appear ;
And feel how light the labors prove,
That follow in the path of Love.

In Thee believing, we rejoice—
    For Thee we watch, we strive, we pray—
Through the dim twilight hear Thy voice,
    As Life's dark shadows flee away ;
Nor ever from our vigils cease,
Until we rest with Thee in peace.

---

## WHAT IS LIFE?

I SAW him in the morn of life,
    A noble, generous one —

Floating his barque on pleasure's sea,
    As honor steered it on—
The breath of hope had swelled the sails,
    And sunshine o'er it hung—
Away it sped its dazzling course,
    While carelessly he sung—

    Oh ! life has naught but happiness—
        Whate'er the wise may say—
    Its freshness and its bloom from me
        Can never pass away.

I saw him then at summer eve,
    He bent his head to hear
The scarcely uttered words which fell
    Like music on his ear;
A lovely girl had murmured them,
    As on his arm she hung,
And radiant was the lover's face
    As once again he sung—

    Oh ! life has naught, etc., etc.

I saw them both again, and she
    Was trembling at his side,
And solemn were the words by which
    He claimed her as his bride.
A crowd of friends were gathered round,
    But to his ear there sprung

A strain his lips had often breathed
   When joyously he sung—

      Oh! life has naught, etc., etc.

I saw his happy home—his wife
   Was o'er an infant bent,
Who, to his matchless smile, a look
   Of answering beauty sent;
He gazed upon the scene, as if
   His earthly hopes were flung
Upon these frail and gentle ones—
   And then once more he sung—

      Oh! life has naught, etc., etc.

I saw a mourner stand alone
   Beside a marble tomb;
One flower was taken in the bud,
   The other in its bloom—
And to the cherished spot he brought
   A heart by sorrow wrung,
But a watch was kept by angels there,
   And thus the spirits sung—

      Oh! life has many a bitter cup—
        Whate'er the young may say—
      But the glory and the peace of Heaven
        Will never pass away.

## *THE RIVER OF LIFE.*

" I STOOD beside a noble stream,
   Whose crystal waters roll'd
Far onward to the distant sea,
   In majesty untold ;
No poisonous herb or deadly fruit
   Grew on that river's brink,
But safely in the tall trees' shade
   The traveller paused to drink."


I saw a man of passions fierce,
   Pass by in bitter mood—
He bent him o'er the cooling wave,
   His anger was subdued ;
And he who ne'er had bowed the knee,
   Now pardon sought of Heaven,
And prayed for blessings on his foes,
   As he would be forgiven.


And then an aged miser came,
   Dreaming of hoarded gold—
Spurning the poor whose humble cry
   Their tale of sorrow told.
He drank ; his rigid hand unclaspt,
   And all his wealth did seem
Too poor an offering for that love
   Which gave a life for him.

I looked again—a widowed form
  Bowed down with grief drew nigh ;
The seal of woe was on her brow,
  And tears had dimm'd her eye.
She took the cup, and hope and joy
  Now filled her grateful heart,
And "we will meet again," she said,
  " Where friends no more shall part."


I could not turn my gaze away,
  And strange it were to tell
The many wondrous miracles
  Wrought by that river's spell !
The young forsook the halls of mirth,
  And with a steadfast eye
The herald of the Cross went forth
  To suffer and to die.


At length I heard a voice—I turned—
  An angel form was near—
I trembled, as in gentle tones
  He said, " Why gaze ye here ?
That river is the Stream of Life,
  On you its power may fall ;
Go drink of its exhaustless wave
  And freely give to all."

## GIDEON'S FLEECE.

A M I, thy meanest servant, Lord,
   To be my country's stay?
To scatter back the Gentile horde
   That rush upon their prey?
These things are far too wonderful
   For a weak heart like mine;
Oh! strengthen now my wavering faith
   And bless me with a sign.
I lay the fleece upon the floor,
   Wilt Thou be ever nigh?
Then let it, Lord, be wet with dew,
   And all the earth be dry.


Once more forgive the daring thought,
   And grant my earnest prayer—
For what were Israel's armies, Lord,
   And Israel's God not there?
Thou who didst guide our fathers through
   The pathless wilderness—
Still, with their children be—and here
   Thy waiting servant bless.
Again this night I spread the fleece,
   Wilt Thou be ever nigh?
Then let the earth be wet with dew,
   The fleece alone be dry.

Christian! the lesson is thine own—
And wouldst thou have a sign?
To know when warring with thy foes,
If Israel's God be thine?
When cloudless skies are o'er thy head,
Nor warning may'st thou trace—
Still in thy heart, with dew from Heaven,
Nourish the plant of grace.
And when affliction's storm shall lower,
And life's rude seas run high—
That heart borne high above the wave
Shall still in faith be dry.

## HOW FAR IS IT TO CANAAN?

HOW far is it to Canaan?
  The way is lone and drear,
Night's shadows darken o'er my path;
  Oh! that my home were near.
Throughout life's weary journey
  My guilt has worn me down;
Shall I e'er reach the promised land
  Or wear the promised Crown?
" Look up, thou fainting one, thy Lord
  This message sends to thee,"
I will blot out thy sins and thou
  " Strong in My strength shall be."

How far is it to Canaan?
  I long to be at home,
Even now the glories of that world
  Over my spirit come.
I see the Heavenly City,
  Its music fills my ear,
Impatient, Lord, I wait, until
  Thy messenger appear.
" Go on, triumphant Christian, yet
  One warning word be given,
Take care, lest too securely trod,
  The road is lost to Heaven."

How far is it to Canaan?
  My treasures all are there,
Flowers of such loveliness had made
  An earthly house too fair.
Mine eyes are dimm'd with weeping,
  I'm desolate and lone,
Yet, Lord! I bless Thy chastening hand,
  Thou didst but take Thine own.
" Mourner, thy trials safely past,
  Now hear thy Saviour say,
I will restore the lost again,
  Where tears are wiped away."

How far is it to Canaan?
  Surely my footsteps tread
Upon the verge of that dark vale
  Before each pilgrim spread.

Whose hand thus leads me onward,
   With strength no more my own?
Father! 'tis Thine, each pledge redeemed,
   I am not left alone.
" Now, soldier, lay thine armor down,
   Sweetly this life resign;
Thy Saviour bore death's sting away,
   And victory is thine."

## *I AM NOT WILLING YET TO DIE.*

" Thy people shall be made willing in the day of Thy power."—
PSALM CX.

I AM not willing yet to die,—
   The earth is green, the sky is fair,
The waters murmur gently by,
   Music and light are everywhere;
The evening breeze, rich with the breath
   Of summer roses, fans my brow;
Withdraw thine icy hand, oh, Death!
   Some other time—not now, not now.

I am not willing yet to die,—
   Autumn has spread such glory round,
Painted our valley gorgeously,
   And every hill with splendor crowned;

Thrown o'er each cliff a crimson wreath,
  Reflected in the lake below—
Withdraw thine icy hand, oh, Death !
  Some other time—not now, not now.

I am not willing yet to die,—
  Our fireside is a joyous one,
And while the wintry storm sweeps by,
  More tender is each loving tone ;
I cannot leave this glowing hearth,
  To lay me down mid frost and snow,
Withdraw thine icy hand, oh, Death !
  Some other time—not now, not now.

I am not willing yet to die,—
  Oh ! look upon the laughing Spring,
While her fair sponsor, Hope, stands by,
  And pledges life to every thing ;
All nature weaves a fragrant wreath
  Of early flowers, to twine her brow—
Withdraw thine icy hand, oh, Death !
  Some other time—not now, not now.

I am not willing yet to die,—
  Alas ! *my time* would never come,
Each changing season adds a tie
  To bind me to my earthly home :
Thou who didst die on Calvary,
  Oh ! make me willing by Thy power ;
Trusting, but weak, I cling to Thee,
  Thine be the way, Thine be the hour.

## *EVENING MEDITATIONS.*

" The joy with which a stranger intermeddleth not."

IT was a cloudless night in June,
  The stars to greet the fair young moon,
   Had all like courtiers come ;
Earth's children to their rest had gone,
And the night breeze went murmuring on,
   Rich with the wood's perfume.

I was alone—but Nature there
Opened her book, and pictures fair,
   To one who loved her gave ;—
The mountains piled in masses high,
Threw their bold outline to the sky—
   Their shadow o'er the wave.

And nearer, gardens blooming round,
And swelling hills with verdure crowned,
   Were spread before my view ;
Though dimly seen—yet known so well—
That day had lent the night a spell,
   To trace each line anew.

And yet, long ere an hour passed by,
The landscape faded from my eye,
   And the bright stars alone
Filled my whole soul, entranced each thought—
Till Fancy deepening as she wrought,
   Gave form to every one.

First to my spirit came the loved,
Year after year from earth removed,
   And still by death endeared ;
Those to whose early loveliness,
E'en Memory could not add one grace,
   Who one blest home had shared.


And friends were there, for whom life wove
A wreath of beauty and of love,
   Then, ere the flowers could fade,
On every leaf a seal was set,
" Gone, but not lost "—they blossom yet,
   Undying, undecayed.


Apostles, martyrs, swelled the throng,
And ransomed myriads swept along,
   In garments dazzling white ;
Till the whole Heavens seemed to be
Filled with a glorious Company
   Of angels robed in light.

  .    .    .    .      .    .    .    .

That hour, that scene, have passed away—
Yet, blest illusion—stay, oh ! stay—
   O'er this dull heart of mine ;
When Faith is dim, and Hope is weak,
Then bid thy shining memories speak
   Of Heaven and things divine.

## THE CHANGELESS MONITOR.

" WHERE art thou going—whence art thou
        come ?
Born with creation, hast thou a home ?
The wind breathes a song in its rushing flight ;
The sun writes a story in burning light ;
But viewless and noiseless thy car moves on,
And men call thee ' Time,' till thy course is run.

" Sapping the strongholds of life away ;
  Touching its grandeur with slow decay ;
  Leading our joys to glad fruition ;
  Healing our sorrows with gentle mission ;
  Making our rapture and grief thy own ;
  Say, is this all, till thy course is run ?

" Borne by thee to a distant shore
  Where thou, and thy dial, are known no more.
  What is the message that we may trace
  In the mystic characters on its face,
  Every throb of our heart's beating
  Still to its fairy round repeating.

" Youth is the questioner; be thou true ;
  Little has age with thee to do.
  His tottering footsteps soon must wait
  Thy last farewell at eternity's gate."

" Mine, has been from distant ages
   All the gathered lore of sages ;
   Mine, are countless hoards of treasure
   Filled up, heaped up—without measure ;
   Mine, the grasp of kingly power ;
   Mine, the victor's proudest hour.

" Mine, the pride of beauty, leading
   Hearts (like captive princes, bleeding
   At a heathen triumph) knowing
   Naught of care for their undoing ;
   Artist work, and poet's rhymes,
   Wedding bells, and victory chimes.

" All of earthly riches, glory,
   Learning, fame in song and story ;
   All are given to me, and I
   Write upon them, ' Vanity.'
   Gleams at most of fitful light—
   Meteors o'er a troubled night.

" Yet, momentous gifts bestowing,
   Life or death, my hand is sowing.
   Gifts of moments—gifts of hours—
   Vested with immortal powers—
   Ever bearing on from me,
   Records for eternity.

" What if the whole world obtaining
   And thy soul is lost, the gaining ?

4

What if registered 'esteeming
Light the price of thy redeeming'?
Open is thy record yet,
Read, where I my seal have set.


" Mark this well; 'a deathless treasure
Lost in giddy rounds of pleasure.'
Here, 'The poisonous goblet tasted,
Youth, and health, and reason wasted.'
Here (the darkest path e'er trod),
  'The fool hath said, there is no God.'


" Here, 'The miser's grip grew tighter.'
Here, 'The idler's mirth grew lighter.'
Here, 'The undying soul, believing
In a great "hereafter," living
One with passion, toil, and strife,
Crushing all of nobler life.'


" Thou art answered.   Pleasures tasted,—
Business thrall,—and moments wasted ;—
   All the good that thou art doing—
All the evil, thou pursuing—
In the characters I trace,
Soon shall meet thee, face to face.


" Not like these be thy recording ;
Not like theirs, thy last awarding ;

Circling years are pausing never—
Soon we part, and part forever—
Then may thy rich guerdon be,
Joyful to remember me."

---

## OUR FATHER IN HEAVEN.

FROM green-clad earth, from sandy shore,
  Where ocean sleeps or tempests roar;
Where the bright river lifts on high
Its waves to greet the circling sky,
Father of Light and Life to Thee,
One chord through all immensity,
Thrills with the tones of need and fear—
Tones quick to reach a father's ear.

Nor dies the infant's feeble wail
In plaintive sighs along the gale;
Nor falls the penitential prayer
Unheeded on the passing air;
The gasp of want—the bitter cry
Born of a love that cannot die,
Are not too poor for Thee to own
Amid the splendors of Thy throne.

Who that in childhood oft might speak
With tearful eye and flushing cheek,

Some tale of wrong, or doubt, or fear,
Into the earthly parent's ear,
(However else the world may prove
Chary of sympathy and love)
But knows his heart may safely rest
Upon a loving father's breast.

And when to Thee our spirits rise
Laden with earth's anxieties;
When from our side the loved are torn,
And faith is dim, and hope forlorn;
When heavy with the dews of night
Our drooping wings scarce seek the light;
How sweet to soothe our griefs to rest
Upon a loving Father's breast.

Nor only thus: by error driven
Too oft we wander far from Heaven;
Too often dazzled by the ray
Of prosperous sunshine, miss the way;
Temptation's warfare fierce within
Goading the soul to doubt and sin;
Repentant, then, still may we rest
Upon a loving Father's breast.

The birds exulting through the air,
Ring out their praises for His care;
The lilies clothed in beauty yield
Their fragrant incense from the field;

But we for whom He sent His Son
To seek the lost,—to save His own,
Alone are called our cares to rest
Upon a loving Father's breast.

His own—though weak in heart and faith—
His own in life—His own in death,
Though here by fires of suffering tried—
Only as silver purified,
Faint not—thy Father lives and reigns,
And every tear that He ordains
Is but a messenger of love
To lead you to His rest above.

. . . . . . . . .

Now, then, as children let us come—
With Thee is peace, and rest, and home ;
Resisting sin, unvexed by strife,
Trusting, amid the toils of life ;
Till Satan conquered, we lay down
Our earthly cross to wear a crown,
And all our sorrows find their rest,
Father, upon Thy loving breast.

## *"HALLOWED BE THY NAME."*

GLORIOUS in strength and majesty,
We hallow Thy great Name ;

The starlit Heavens—the teeming earth,
  Its wondrous power proclaim.
Imprinted on the mountain crest,
  The torrent's ceaseless flow;
Nor less on every fluttering leaf
  And wayside flower below.

The child scarce passed from infancy
  Sees in his father's hand
A power that he would vainly wield,
  Would vainly understand;
Yet not for this unfailing trust
  And filial reverence meet;
But for the tender care that guides
  His feeble, tottering feet.

And He who leads the lightning flash
  Along its fiery path;
Who binds at will the stormy winds,
  The surging waters' wrath,
Still makes our human griefs His own—
  Our wandering steps can stay;
And from the splendors of His throne
  Wipes all our tears away.

Father! what offering can we bring
  That is not Thine to claim?
Oh! for a seraph's raptured strains
  To magnify Thy Name.

Not where an angel veils his face
  May mortal vision soar;
Only with childlike trust and love
  We praise Thee evermore.


And though our words be few and weak,
  Our hearts oft ill at ease,
Now idly drifting with the wave—
  Now breasting stormy seas;
With Thee is rest—all else may change,
  But Thou art still the same;
And with Thy works we magnify
  And hallow Thy great Name.


## "*AND WHEN HE THOUGHT THEREON, HE WEPT.*"—MARK xiv. 72.

" AND when He thought thereon, He wept."
    Alas! alas! too late the tears!
O memories of the past that kept
  Their sleepless watch through coming years!


He sees the fisher's garb he wore,
  His boat rocks idly on the sea;
Mending his net upon the shore
  He hears the summons, "Follow Me."

Can he forget the pitying love
   That healed the soul He came to bless,
The heart all human woe could move
   To ministry of tenderness?

The cry—the bitter, anguished cry
   That rose above the stormy wave—
The Master's whisper, "It is I,"
   The Master's hand outstretched to save.

And was it he, of all that band,
   Who would for his dear Lord have died,
O coward heart! O feeble hand!
   O traitor tongue, his Lord denied.

His Lord forsaken of His own,
   Led to betrayal with a kiss;
Buffeted, mocked, and spit upon,
   Was ever sorrow like to His?

One look He gave! the flood-gates gone,
   Onward the surging billows swept;
Grief and remorse must claim their own,
   "And when He thought thereon, He wept."

———

Oh! heart of mine, how oft hast thou
   Pleading for self, thy Lord denied;
Canst thou forget the thorn-crowned brow,
   The wounded hands, the bleeding side,

The shadows of Gethsemane,
  The agonizing watch He kept
For thee, O faithless heart, for thee—
  And hast thou "thought thereon and wept"?

---

## *BARTIMEUS.*

### MARK x. 46.

"HE is coming! He is coming! I hear along
      the street
The sound of many voices—the tread of many
      feet!
Is it the man of Nazareth—the man I heard you
      say,
That healed the sick, and raised the dead—and
      will He pass this way?

"Why would ye bid me hold my peace—who else
      my life can save
From darkness heavier than the night, more
      hopeless than the grave;
For you, the blessed sun may shine—for you, the
      earth is fair;
But earth and sunshine bring to me the black-
      ness of despair."

From the dimmed caverns of the brain, a cry has
    come for light ;
The struggle of a human soul, thirsting for human
    sight ;
That cry is heard, the sufferer's hope—the suf-
    ferer's only plea—
" Jesus, Thou Son of David, have mercy upon me !"

His steps are stayed—upon the throng a stillness
    falls like death,
The Son of Man, in Godlike power, has quelled
    the tumult's breath ;
And words of pity pierce the air—"Arise, and go
    thy way."
" Thy faith hath saved thee," morning breaks and
    night is lost in day.

He turned and followed Jesus ! so love is born
    of faith,
No more a beggar asking alms, along the way-
    side path ;
The glory of the earth is His—the sunshine and
    the flowers,
And songs of love, and songs of joy—O, happy,
    happy hours !

Blind—blind, as Bartimeus, in prison bonds held
    down,
" Raking up straws, while overhead, an angel
    bears a crown."*

    * Bunyan's " Pilgrim's Progress,"—the man with the muck-rake.

A human soul from darkness is struggling to be
    free—
"Jesus, Thou Son of David, have mercy upon
    me."

## *"LIKEWISE JOY SHALL BE IN HEAVEN."*

LUKE XV. 3-10.

" SAY, shepherd, whither goest thou,
    Scaling with eager feet
The dark and treacherous mountain-path
    Mid storm, and snow, and sleet?
Thine eye would vainly seek to pierce
    The gathering gloom of night;
Thy flock is sheltered—rest thee here—
    Our cottage fires burn bright."

" Delay me not—ninety and nine
    Are safe within the fold,
Nor tell me that the way is lone,
    And pitiless the cold;
For one poor wanderer treads the verge
    Of yonder black abyss,
And I must seek and save the lost
    From such a death as this."

" Go, shepherd, on thy Heaven-taught quest
    Of pity and of love,

Until the songs of men rejoice
  With angel songs above;
Until the erring, storm-wrecked soul
  Once more be homeward bound;
Until thy dead shall live again—
  Until thy lost be found."

Who tends the Master's flock, full well
  The Master's Cross doth know,
For he must scale the frowning rock,
  Must bridge the depths below;
Must homeward lead the wounded soul
  With tender, pitying love.
So shall the songs of men rejoice
  With angel songs above.

## RETROSPECTION.

M ANY years have passed away
    Since a well-remembered day
When beneath a lilac bloom,
Revelling in rich perfume,
Following out a childish thought,
I, the lowly blossoms sought,
Myrtle—heartsease—violet—
In the shadowy frame-work set.

Still I seem a child again
Fearing nought of grief or pain,
Only on my quest intent—
Only on my treasure bent—
In a blissful fairy land,
Reaching out a dimpl'd hand,
When a rude and startling grasp,
Strong of will and firm of clasp,
While the tender flesh was torn,
Pierced with many a cruel thorn—
Snatched me from the leafy bower
Half bereft of life and power,
Strange the work that love had done—
Strange the trophy love had won !


" Father, was the hand Thy own ? "
Wept my heart with bitter moan ;
Still His voice is in my ear—
" Saw thou not the Serpent near ? "


Through the mists of after years
Reproduced from blinding tears,
With a quick, keen sense of pain
Came the picture back again.
" Father, is the hand Thy own ? "
Pleads my heart with bitter moan,
And the answer meets my ear—
" Saw thou not the Serpent near ? "

Children still, through careless hours
Ever seeking fragrant flowers,
Wandering with unwary feet,
Where the bloom and shadow meet,
Does a Father's watchful eye
Rescue thee from danger nigh,
Pleads thy heart with bitter moan,
" Father, is the hand Thy own ? "
Let the answer meet thy ear,
" Saw thou not the Serpent near ? "

---

## GALILEE.

### MATT. iv. 23.

THE storied hills of Galilee
   Are bright with blooming flowers,
And waters on the restless sea
   Flash through the sunlit hours ;
And Childhood's happy voice is there,
   And Youth in morning's prime,
And Age that marks with hoary hair
   The dial-plate of Time.

But Childhood flings its roses by,
   And Youth forgets its song,
And feeble Age, with eager eye,
   Moves restlessly along ;

From hill and plain they throng—they press,
  And on the glittering sands
Only a youth of lowly dress,
  But noble presence, stands.

A King—He came unto His own,
  His own received Him not!
A King discrowned—without a throne—
  And toil His daily lot:
And on the sea, and on the shore,
  His Presence stills the air,
And words man never spake before
  Hold waiting thousands there.

As shadows tell the waning day,
  Low kneeling at His feet,
The sore distressed their burdens lay
  And all their woes repeat.
O Love Divine that came to bear
  Our Cross of shame and pain,
For even the outcast leper there
  Could never plead in vain.

Lights stream from palace windows now,
  And odors faint and sweet,
Where will He cool His fevered brow,
  Where rest His weary feet?
A royal Prince—no welcome said
  To Him from princely hall;

He hath not where to lay His head,
　　And He is Lord of all.

Land of the olive and the vine,
　　Where is thy grandeur now?
Thy children's sin and woe are thine,
　　Their curse is on thy brow.
And sons and daughters, exiled, toil
　　Through scorn, and grief, and loss,
While alien footprints mark the soil
　　They shadowed with the Cross.

O storied hills of Galilee,
　　Long desolate and lone,
The waters of thy restless sea
　　For thee make ceaseless moan ;
And Gentile hordes with ruthless hand
　　Thy fairest gifts lay waste,
And all the glory of thy land
　　Sleeps in the buried past.

Sleep is not death !　Thy King shall come
　　In triumph from the skies ;
Thy vine-clad slopes in beauty bloom,
　　Thy palace splendors rise.
Legions of angels round Him now
　　His royal state maintain,
And every knee to Him shall bow,
　　Whose right it is to reign.

## *ANNIE.*

" And they sung as it were a new song."—Rev. xiv. 3.
" These are they which follow the Lamb whithersoever he goeth.
These were redeemed from among men, being the first fruits unto
God and the Lamb."—Rev. xiv. 4.

SAY, canst thou bear her a message?
   Thy spirit is winging its flight
To a land that she entered before thee,
   All radiant with glory and light;
And when at His feet whom thou lovest,
   Thy lips shall breathe forth a new song,
With the angels adoring around thee,
   Her voice the glad note shall prolong.

Say, canst thou bear her a message?
   She was our *first-born*—our beloved,—
A few years she lingered among us,
   And then the fair child was removed;
So lovely, dost thou not remember
   The wave of her soft, golden hair?
So gentle, so pure, so unearthly—
   We know that our darling is there.

Tell her that earth has no blessing
   Her loss in our hearts to supply,
That the Grief-opened fount closes never!
   That Sorrow's dark stream runs not dry!

5

But the Cross that our Master has hallowed,
    Must still to His servants be dear,
And the false world no more can allure us
    To dream that our treasures are here.

Tell her, while memory wakens
    One thought of the past, she is ours—
She comes with all visions of beauty,
    She has left a new charm for the flowers;
The sunset, the starry night's splendor,
    The summer eve's murmuring close,
And see thou forget not to tell her,
    We love for her sake "the white rose."

Say, canst thou bear her a message?
    Thy spirit is winging its flight—
One word which the earth cannot sully,
    Go sound through the regions of light;
'Tis the name of the Lord, our Redeemer,
    That name to her young heart so dear,
And tell her, her Saviour is precious
    To those she left sorrowing here!

---

## A CHRISTMAS-DAY LETTER.

AH! my heart is weary!
    Let me charm its grief away
Every pulse vibrating,
    To the Angels' song to-day.

Hark the pealing anthem,
With Time alone to cease,—
" Hail ! Thou Infant Saviour !
Hail ! Thou Prince of Peace !

Once, the household idol,
Her gentle beauty blest,
Amid the showering roses
Of the spring-time, found her rest ;
And yesterday, beside her,
We laid a darling one ;
Our two years' pet and plaything—
A sunbeam, come and gone.

Ah ! our hearts are weary !
Let us charm our grief away ;
Their voices join the chorus
Of the Angels' song, to-day ;
And we, adoring, catch the anthem,
With Time alone to cease,—
" Hail ! Thou Infant Saviour !
Hail ! Thou Prince of Peace ! "

Peace ! Alas ! around us
Everywhere is strife ;
Brother against brother,
Hunting life for life,
Gloom and desolation
Brood o'er many a hearth,

Ringing once with laughter—
Wild with childish mirth.

Yet amid the fires,
Our Lord still finds His own,
Looking for their deliverance,
In every heart a throne;
And swelling still the anthem,
With Time alone to cease,—
"Hail! Thou Infant Saviour!
Hail! Thou Prince of Peace!"

In the Heavenly City,
When from golden harp-strings rung,
"As the voice of many waters,"
The glad "New Song" is sung,
The redeemed shall wake an anthem,
No more with Time to cease,—
"Hail! Thou risen Saviour!
Hail! Thou Prince of Peace!"

*December* 25, 1864.

## THE ANGEL VISITANT.

"Are they not all ministering spirits?"

TREAD softly!
The toil and strife of the day are done,—
Soft falls the glow of the setting sun.

Fling wide the doors, where the joyous ring
Of the heart's rich music is echoing.
Wide—for an Angel guest is come,
Unbidden, unmark'd to the happy home;
Flowers are blooming everywhere,
Life's purest flowers are blooming there.

Tread softly!
  The hours pass on to another rest,
  'Mid the parting glory that fills the west;
  Heavy and dark are the mists that rise,
  Veiling its light from anxious eyes;
  They see not the Angel with noiseless wing,—
  They knew not his gentle entering;
  Shadows are falling everywhere,—
  Life's deepest shadow is falling there.

Tread softly!
  The hours pass on to another rest,
  And sunset flushes the glowing west;
  Silently kneel, where the sufferer lies,
  With a heavenly light in her dreamy eyes.
  Kneel, for the Angel with noiseless wing
  To the rapt spirit is ministering;
  "Passing away," is on all things fair,—
  Passing forever from earth, is there!

Tread softly!
  The hours pass on to another rest,
  And twilight fades in the darkening west;

Strength, to the stricken, has come with death—
Strength, that is born of unbroken faith,—
And the Angel guest, with noiseless wing,
O'er the wounded in spirit is hovering.
Shadows are falling everywhere,—
Light and shadow are falling there.

Tread softly !
Hush'd and still is the dewy eve,
Where the beloved to rest they leave.
What though the desolate heart is worn,
One, on the Cross, hath its burden borne ;
And still to their sorrow, with healing wing,
His angels are ever ministering ;
Blessings are falling everywhere,—
A blessing of peace is falling there.

## "*IN THY PRESENCE.*"

" I AM wandering here in darkness,
        I am weary of the night,
Faith would vainly pierce the distance
        To my Father's home of light,
Where one glad, glorious morning
        Ushers in Eternal Day,
And earthly clouds and shadows
        Forever flee away.

" I am weary of the conflicts
    That my halting steps pursue,
Of the foes so lately vanquished
    Ever springing up anew ;
Of the cumbrous, glittering armor
    At eve laid down in pain,
And, with the first awaking,
    To be girded on again.

" I am weary of the weeping,
    Of bereavement's darkened life ;
Of the want and desolation—
    Of the toil and pain and strife ;
Of the hollow show and seeming
    Of a world by sin oppressed,
I am weary—I am weary—
    And I long to be at rest ! "

" Art thou weary of My service ?
    Is thy love so cold to Me ?
In thy trials, thy temptations,
    Have I weary been of thee ?
The path that thou must follow
    I have trod with bleeding feet,
And if the *toil* be bitter,
    Will not the *rest* be sweet ? "

" Lord, forgive my weak repining !
    Fellow-travellers in the way

Wounded by sin and sorrow,
   Nor Priest nor Levite stay;
Teach me to win them homeward,
   The lost—the blind—the lame,
My feeble work accepted
   In Thy beloved Name.

'Onward ever at Thy bidding,
   Though the path be lone and drear,
Only let me trace Thy footprints,
   Only feel that Thou art near;
Till o'er the waters gleaming
   Falls the light from yonder shore,
'In Thy Presence there is fullness
   Of joy forevermore.'"

## A FRAGMENT.

A GLORY floods Judea,
   As sunlight floods the sea:
Shepherds, who watch your flocks by night,
   What may this glory be?
While Eve her many voices hushed
   Drinks in with ravished ear
The song by angels brought to earth—
   That earth no more may hear.

That glory from past ages
  By prophet vision seen,
Though dimly gleaming through the night,
  A star of hope had been—
That song which kings had waited for
  In echoings sublime,
Shall still the wondrous story tell
  Down to the verge of time.

---

## *THE THIRD SUNDAY IN ADVENT.*

" It is required in stewards that a man be found faithful."—1
COR. iv. 2.

OH ! life is but a pilgrimage, and every traveller
    bears,
Whate'er his state—where'er his way—the bur-
    den of its cares ;
For Pleasure's fountains ever gleam where Sor-
    row's shade is thrown,
And he who fills the sparkling cup shall find them
    both his own.

Deeply upon the poor man's brow the seal of care
    is set,
And heavily it presses with the kingly coronet ;

Then ye who feed the Saviour's flock, like Him
    each day go forth,
And minister in mercy to the suffering ones of
    earth.

Like Him, thou bearest messages of love to every
    heart—
Like Him, the bread of life thou may'st freely to
    all impart;
And if thy work be hidden long, faint not, nor be
    dismayed.
Thou canst not weep as He hath wept, nor pray
    as He hath prayed.

Oh! Holy office! thus to watch for the undying
    soul—
To whisper gentle words of peace where passion's
    billows roll,
To break the spell of careless mirth—the droop-
    ing spirit cheer,
When sad bereavement clouds the home, that
    else had been too dear.

And did He not His tender lambs give to thy
    watchful care?
For precious in the Shepherd's sight the young
    and feeble are.
We cannot know how brief a span of life to these
    is given,
E'en now their infant feet may stand just at the
    gate of Heaven.

Then guard them well, for memory brings oft to
    the grateful breast
The last hours of a little child thus early laid to
    rest ;
Her pastor's name was on her lips, and to his
    hand she gave
A token of revering love that dies not in the
    grave.

Oh! be thou faithful to thy trust, a rich reward
    is thine—
Forever and forever, as the glorious stars to
    shine—
And the chief Shepherd in thy crown no brighter
    gems may weave,
Than they who by thy teachings here like little
    children live.

## " THE FASHION OF THIS WORLD PASSETH AWAY."

BEAUTY, with her handmaids fair,
    Hover'd o'er the infant earth,
Showering fragrance through the air,
    Waking loveliness to birth.
With her wand she tinged the flowers,
    Curtained Heaven's high arch with blue,

Pencilled clouds for evening hours,
  Gave the morn its rosy hue;

Robed in mist the lofty mountain,
  Softly veiled the dewy plain;
Decked with light the crystal fountain,
  Lost in forest depths again;
On the lake's calm bosom mirrored,
  Starry jewels of the night;
Through all nature still untired,
  Blending color, shade, and light.

Now Creation's full harp swelling,
  To each note she lent its tone;
One task more, all else excelling,
  Ere her work of love is done;
Shadowy land and sparkling water,
  This last gift is not for thee,
But to throw o'er Eden's daughter
  Perfect grace and symmetry.
One there followed in her train,
  With an aspect coldly stern;
Beauty saw and wept in vain.
  Wheresoe'er her footsteps turn,
Still that stranger form is near—
  "And who art thou?" she said,
"And wherefore art thou here?"

    Not a word spoke the stranger,
      But in his grasp glittered

A seal, and the motto was,
  " Passing away."
And all that was lovely
  These sad words embittered ;
And deeply he stamped
  Where the loveliest lay.

Then Beauty, with sorrow
  And tenderness riven,
Her fair maidens gathered,
  And homeward took flight ;
Children of earth,
  Ye may meet her in Heaven ;
At the fount of Perfection
  She feareth no blight.

---

*" COME UNTO ME, ALL YE."*—Matt. xi. 28.

COME where the Sun of Righteousness is
    throwing
A glow of radiance o'er life's clouded way ;
Come where that Sun its guiding light bestowing
  Points on to brighter realms of endless day.

Come, all that labor and are heavy laden,
  I will refresh you with my Spirit's power ;
The promised bloom of life is ever fading,
  But I will lead where joys eternal flower.

A bruised reed, a broken, contrite spirit
  May rest its cares and sufferings safely here;
On earth, a Saviour's griefs though it inherit,
  In Heaven is wept away each bitter tear.


Come *now*—nor slight the gracious invitation
  Which says to every weary traveller, Come,
Here is for all a balm of Consolation—
  And I will bid each wanderer welcome home.


## THE VOICE OF THE GRAVE.

WHEN will ye wake again,
    Oh! lovely slumberers in the silent
        tomb?
  Can ye not burst the chain
That holds ye fettered in Corruption's gloom?
Can ye not rise to life and light once more,
And eyes now dimmed with grief to joy restore?


  Spring flowers are wafting on
The first soft perfume of the early year,
  And many a warbling tone
By the small bird, is waked in forest drear;
See *ye* the woods with fragrant blossoms crowned?
Hear *ye* the harmony that breathes around?

When will ye wake again?
Voice of the sepulchre deep-toned and low,
Long have we watched in vain!
Speak! to our hearts thy hidden mysteries show
Tell us,—we laid the pale fair sleepers here:
We call them now—when will the loved appear?

Call back the tint of yonder fading rose—
Call up the dew at summer evening shed—
Call back the light yon darting meteor throws—
*Then* call ye back the dead.

Call back the wave on yonder ocean's breast—
Call up the moonbeams from their glassy bed,
As on the rippling lake they gently rest—
*Then* call ye back the dead.

Call back the mighty winds that sweep along—
Call back the fading cloud, at sunset spread—
Call back the thunder's voice, fearful and strong—
*Then* call ye back the dead.

Yet, they shall waken from their dreamless sleep—
Hearest thou the Archangel's pealing trumpet
sound?
" Earth, now give up thy dead "—" Oh! soundless
deep,
Give back the forms in death's cold fetters
bound;

Awake ! Awake !" Lone slumberers in the
     tomb,
Thy chain is broke—rouse from Corruption's
     gloom.

-----

## *THE MISSIONARY'S DEATH-BED.*

IT was not in her own bright home,
     Where clustering vines and bowers,
Scattered rich fragrance with the bloom
     Of summer's bending flowers ;
Or where the loved were met in prayer
     At evening, side by side ;
Her childhood's blessed home was there,
     But 'twas not there she died.

It was not on her mother's breast
     She laid her wearied head ;
But strange and swarthy beings pressed
     Around the sufferer's bed.
And there fell many a bitter tear
     And many a soothing tone,
Although no kindred voice was near
     To cheer the dying one.

Her cheek was flushed with fever's heat,
     Its light was in her eye,

As memory many a picture drew
　From thoughts that wandered by ;
And from her parted lips some words
　In murmured accents spoke—
A tone from feeling's quivering chord,
　Just thrilling as they broke.

.　　.　　.　　.　　.　　.　　.　　.　　.

Mother, it is your child, give me your hand—
And my sweet sister, too—a lovely band
Of gentle spirits gathered round me now
To wipe the death-chill from my aching brow.
It is long since I have seen you—and I feared
Ye would not come in time—but I was heard,
Even in that half-breathed prayer—oh ! mother,
　　raise
For all *His* mercies one glad song of praise.

It breathes upon my heart of feelings won
From dark oblivion's shadows—every tone
Tells of some early pleasure—now my ear
Drinks in the music I have loved to hear.
In my own native land—the hum of bees—
The song of warbling birds swells on the breeze—
The laughing voice of childhood as we played
In careless mirth, under the tall trees' shade.

Was it a dream ?　Is this my happy home ?
Was it my mother's voice, amid death's gloom
6

Speaking of peace ?    Alas ! why dream I still ?
Oh ! Father, bend Thy servant to Thy will.
My spirit is exhausted—and the light
Of earthly ties receding from my sight.
Lift my dimm'd gaze to Thee, Thou blessed One,
'Mid the unfading splendors of Thy throne.


Thy love's refreshing moisture on my head
Has fallen like dew at summer evening shed—
And even while in the agony of death
Thy Spirit will be with me ; now my breath
Is quick and short ; my feeble pulse just gone—
But Thou art here ; I am not left alone.
Come, quickly come—lend me Thy wings of love—
Oh ! for the soaring pinions of the dove,
That I might flee away and be at rest
With Thee, my God, my Father, first and blest !
I see Thee now—the sting of death is past—
Oh ! precious Saviour ! home—at last—at last !


Far in a distant Southern land
   Her resting-place they made—
By India's spicy breezes fann'd,
   Beneath the palm-tree's shade—
And o'er her grave one sorrowing heart
   Wept desolate and lone—
Oh, Death ! 'tis ever thine to part
   Those Love on earth made one.

## THE SOUL'S BAZAAR.

" Remember that thou in thy lifetime receivedst THY good things."—LUKE xvi. 25.

WHAT an assemblage ! what a vast crowd !
    Some pressing eagerly, clamorous, and
        loud,
Others pass onward with purposes high,
A " will " in the heart, and resolve in the eye ;
The lover of gold, and the lover of pleasure,—
The beauty—the priest—each to barter for treas-
        ure—
    And each for himself—for the bond that is given
    Can only be cancelled in Hell or in Heaven.

Here is wealth for the miser, stocks, houses, and
        lands—
He may pave from his coffers the ground where
        he stands ;
But the generous current of life must run dry ;
It must dwindle each day till it fade from the eye ;
It must flow on through sands, where the sun's
        scorching heat
On the head of the traveller unsheltered shall beat,
Leaving far in the distance the freshening shade,
And the song of the bird in the green forest glade,
With a grip for the widow—a deaf ear to the cry
Of the poor and the fatherless ! Say, who will buy ?

For your pledge you may take—but the bond
      that is given
Can only be cancelled in Hell or in Heaven.


Here is power for the statesman.  But up the
      steep height
Toiling onward by day, toiling onward by night,
He must not grow dizzy nor falter, for "truth"—
He must fling from his path the best friend of his
      youth—
He must talk of "the people," and trade with
      their blood—
His country, himself! and his heaven, bestud
With the stars of *his* greatness! while fished
      from the mire
The "law of his conscience" grows "higher" and
      " higher."
No arousing for him till he wake with the cry,
" The forever lost birthright!" Say, who will buy?
   For your pledge you may take, but the bond
      that is given
   Can only be cancelled in Hell or in Heaven.


Here is wine for the Bacchanal, drink in the bowl,
To gladden the heart, and to madden the soul!
Fill the cup with the vine leaves so gracefully
      crowned—
Hide the serpent within—let the guests gather
      round—

While the senses are steeped, as, now distant,
    now clear,
An exquisite melody thrills on the ear.
Not yet the debauch! From the young and the
    gay,
Come flashes of wit, and the eloquent play
Of feeling and sentiment. Can you withstand
The rapture dealt out with so lavish a hand?
It is bliss for the night—who takes thought for
    the morrow?
Who dreams of repentance—or tampers with
    sorrow?
But the leaf-hidden adder has poisoned the life—
On, on, to the drunkard—the heart-broken wife—
The children, so wronged—and each gift, one by
    one,
All pride and all honor—all intellect, gone.
Who bids now for pleasure? Quick, quick, stocks
    run high,
And sales, too, are brisk. Who will buy—who
    will buy?
  For your pledge you may take, but the bond
    that is given
  Can only be cancelled in Hell or in Heaven.


Here are goods for all time. The "physician"
    may see
Only Nature's great laws in the veiled Deity;
Secure in the trust of an infidel faith,

Content to walk blindfold, while grappling with
　　death.
The " lawyer's " frail justice may trample on
　　" right "—
The coil of the fee bind his conscience at sight.
The " priest " in delusion may leave far aside
The penitent path for the trappings of pride,
And count it all holy—although he has sold
" The Book " for man's wisdom—for tinsel, the
　　gold.
The " beauty " may find in the wrongs she would
　　mete,
Her own lawful tribute just laid at her feet ;
And thoughtless " self-will " the boon it may
　　crave,
Undeterr'd from its mark by the opening grave.
　Each must choose for himself, but the bond
　　that is given
　Can only be cancelled in Hell or in Heaven.


Here ! a " pearl of great price." It is yours on
　　demand.
Would you have the clear head, and the liberal
　　hand, .
The heart that beyond its own selfish concerns
To the need of another untiringly turns,
Integrity, uprightness, honor, and truth,
The crown of old age, and the glory of youth ;
No truckling for station, no penalty paid

For weak self-indulgence in pitiful trade.
With the rich, who so rich !—with the great, who
    so high !
Who so honored to live—so lamented to die
As the man with this " pearl " ?  And as years
    still increase
No dreaded " hereafter " o'ershadows his peace ;
Pass on—but in shipwreck, when breakers run
    high,
You may dream of the past !  Who will buy—who
    will buy ?
    The investment is safe, for the bond that is
    given,
    Accepted on earth, will be cancelled in Heaven.

## WHAT THOUGHTS ARE THINE, FAIR BOY?

[My little brother, while under the influence of high fever, said
to me: "Sister, two of them were dressed in white, and oh ! they
were so pretty !"]

WHAT thoughts are thine, fair boy,
    In that dreamy, restless sleep ?
The visionings before thee now
    May wear a meaning deep.
Thy murmurs are of lovely things—
    Of beings robed in white ;

Say, has thy rest been visited
  By angel forms of light?

The beautiful in spirit
  Have met thy slumbering gaze
Perchance they gather round thy couch,
  The sinking one to raise ;
Perchance they bear a zephyr's breath
  To fan thy flushing cheek,
Or o'er thy fainting heart a tone
  Of cheery hope they speak.

Thou hast of earthly beauty
  In its highest, proudest mould ;
For intellect's rich treasury
  Is on thy forehead told.
And there is language in thine eye,
  With genius deeply fraught,
As kindling high with feeling's warmth,
  Or drooped in pensive thought.

A bud of fairest promise
  Thou hast ever been, sweet one,
But over the expanding bloom
  A shadowing has gone.
The cloud may pass and thou fulfil
  Our dearest hopes on earth,
Or else, removed to brighter climes,
  The bud will blossom forth.

## *THE SECOND TEMPLE.*

" But many of the priests and Levites and chief of the fathers, who were ancient men, that had seen the first house, when the foundation of this house was laid before their eyes, wept with a loud voice ; and many shouted aloud for joy ":

" So that the people could not discern the noise of the shout of joy from the noise of the weeping of the people: for the people shouted with a loud shout, and the noise was heard afar off."— EZRA iii. 12, 13.

A SOUND is heard on Judah's holy hill,
　　Like rushing water, powerful and strong ;
Loud acclamations all the hushed air fill,
　　And proudly swells on high the choral song.
Hark ! hark ! the pealing bursts of triumph rise
Through the wide heavens, piercing the vaulted
　　skies.
　　　．　　．　　．　　．　　．　　．　　．　　．　　．

The harp of Israel long in silence slept,
　　For stilled and powerless was the captive's
　　　hand—
And her fair daughters, once her pride, now wept
　　Their sorrowing bondage in a foreign land.
Her sons—her warrior sons—the mighty free,
Did they, too, languish in captivity ?

Was all the spirit of their fathers dead,
　　That arm to arm defied the giant's power ?
Had all remembrance from their bosoms fled,
　　That they recalled not victory's glorious hour ?

And, spurning chains that bound them to the
      dust,
Rose not once more a few to quell a host?

Alas! one arm that went before that band
    To combat and to conquer, was not there;
The sword of fire, grasped by no mortal hand,
    That bore along its path death and despair;
The hovering cloud—the light that cheered them
        on,
Marking their doubtful way—were all withdrawn.

Daughters of Judah! bend your graceful heads,
    And weep in anguish o'er your country's lot;
Warriors! the light departed glory sheds,
    Your fame—your greatness—all avail you not.
Bow, haughty ones; in dust and ashes mourn.
Call on your God—haply He may return.

That cry was heard: freed from the captive's
        yoke,
    Once more her children stand on Zion's mount;
Then from their hearts a gush of feeling broke,
    Like waters bursting from a long-sealed fount.
On the old hallowed spot once more the cry
Of praise, triumphant praise, ascends on high.

Is there no tone but triumph's swelling there,
    No sound of lamentation borne along?

No mourner's wailing sweeping through the air,
  With the wild echo of exulting song?
Whence come these notes of woe?   Mourner,
    away!
Discordant grief is not for this proud day.

Is it some youthful spirit weeping here—
  The first crushed hope of life's dark pilgrim-
    age?
Oh, no! more touching still; the sorrowing tear
  Is trickling down the furrowed cheek of age.
Fathers in Israel! men with hoary hair,
What touch thus rudely wakes your heart's
    despair?

Alas! it thrills on memory's aching chord,
  And calling forth once more a deathless tone,
That time had lulled, grief's swelling tide is
    poured
  Forth in one deep lament. Old men, weep on—
Weep o'er the record stamped on each green sod,
Of rebel man, and an avenging God.

In one dark mass of ruin all was laid:
  The cherubim whose shadowing wings were
    bent
Over the mercy-seat—the long arcade—
  The high, majestic porch where thousands
    went

To bow in solemn worship at the throne—
The chosen shrine of Israel's Holy One.

Ye saw the former temple in its pride
   Lit with a blaze of gems and fretted gold,
And heard ye not the unsanctified deride
   The Lord of Hosts in His high fane of old ?
Did ye not see destruction's fearful gust
Sweep o'er the walls and lay them in the dust ?

Yet from this wreck of grandeur there shall rise
   Another temple in its towering pride.
But can the light come back to aged eyes,
   Or vigor to the heart when youth has died ?
Oh, no ! that brilliant lamp, once quenched and
     gone,
Relights no more.  Old men, weep on—weep on !

## THE SPIRIT'S HOME.

SPIRIT ! where is thy resting-place
   On the gay and laughing earth ?
Where warbling birds sing merrily
   And flowers blossom forth ?
Or where the young and thoughtless meet,
   In pleasure's glittering hall—
With smiles and gems and roses wreathed
   Decked for the festival ?

Oh! no—oh! no.  The sunlit earth
  In loveliness shall glow—
But 'tis a changeful light, for clouds
  Many dark shadows throw,—
And hopes that spring to cheer the heart
  Are blighted in their birth,
And birds and flowers must pass away—
  My home is not of earth.

Is it upon the Ocean's breast—
  Where tall ships wing their way
And proudly ride the crested waves
  Amid the dashing spray?
Where the wearied sun goes down to rest
  In one broad blaze of light,
And the bosom of the glassy sea
  Reflects the starry night?

Oh! no—oh! no.  The sailor dares
  Old ocean fearlessly—
But many a dauntless heart now sleeps
  Beneath the dark blue sea;
And gallant ships have gone to wreck
  On foaming billows toss'd,
Where the tempest's wing alone might bear
  The death-cry of the lost.

But would ye know my blessed home—
  Go with the eye of faith,

Where storms and tempests never come
  To tell of wreck and death ;
Where withered hopes no more shall rise
  To haunt the troubled breast,
And tears are wiped from weeping eyes,
  And the weary are at rest.

## " *JESUS WEPT.*"

HE wept !   Beside a lowly grave,
  The Lord of Life, the sinless, wept ;
Softly along the distant hills,
  The shadowy hues of evening slept ;
And on the quiet air arose
  A tone of heavenly pity, swept
O'er angel harps from age to age,
  For mortal suffering—" Jesus wept ! "

He wept—nor turned from Mary's tears,
  While kneeling on the hallowed sod.
Her trembling faith but half discerned,
  In human form, the Son of God.
Nor will He scorn a suppliant now—
  For us, Love's ceaseless watch is kept ;
Then lay thy burden at His feet—
  For mortal suffering, " Jesus wept ! "

    .   .   .   .   .   .   .   .   .

" I would we were at rest, dear Lord !
    I would this night of grief were gone !
Our spirits toiling heavily,
    Watch sadly for the coming dawn ;
A night, that with its solemn hush,
    Brings sterner duties than the day:
Night, with no sleep for weary eyes,
    When will its shadows flee away !

" Sharply across the oppressive gloom,
    The ring of battle strikes the ear :
Lord, who will stay the mourner's heart ?
    Lord, who will dry the orphan's tear ?
On every surging billow tossed,
    We cry from the relentless wave ;
'Tis Thine to bend the tempest's wrath,
    'Tis Thine to comfort ! Thine to save ! "

.   .   .   .   .   .   .   .   .

A still, small voice has pierc'd the storm,
    It whispers to my heart of peace :
" Arise, and put thy sins away,
    Nor let thy toil, thy watchings cease.
Loved with an everlasting love,
    I will thy fainting heart renew ;
*Look from thyself*—with every hour,
    There is a work for thee to do.

" Go, tell in camp, on battlefield,
    Of Jesus, who for sinners died ;

Go, bid the penitent behold
   My wounded hands, my bleeding side.
Lone, sick or weary, prison-bound,
   At home, abroad, My people pine;
Tell them their sorrows are My own—
   Was ever human love like Mine?

' Above the cloud that dims thine eyes,
   My hand in all thy chastenings see;
From Me shall thy deliverance come.
   A captive now—thou shalt be free.
O'er every trial, every tear,
   My love its ceaseless watch hath kept;
Then bow with Mary at My feet,
   For her, for thee, thy Lord hath wept!"

*Fast Day, April 8, 1864.*

------

*IN MEMORY OF CADET JOHN QUARLES.*

VIRGINIA MILITARY INSTITUTE.

SHADE from the dawn the falling tear,
   Shut out the glad, rejoicing spring;
What need of earthly sunshine here—
   The light of Heaven is entering:
Angels are come on noiseless wing,
   The sufferer's fainting heart to cheer;

And Heaven's own light is entering—
    What need of earthly sunshine here.

Oh ! glory hidden from our eyes
    Veiled by this frail mortality !
Oh ! cloudless sun ! for *us* to rise
    Never, till death shall set us free !
We wait in awe—in love we watch
    The ransomed spirit's flickering rays ;
And still the ear is strained to catch
    Prayer, soon to be exchanged for praise.

———

" Wash me, my Saviour, make me clean.
    Oh ! cleanse my soul from every stain,
While on Thy loving arm I lean,
    Again—oh ! wash me yet again.

" Wash me, my Saviour—at Thy feet
    I lay the burden of my sin.
Wash me, my Saviour—oh ! complete
    Thy work—my Saviour, wash me clean !

" Not me alone—for *all* I pray ;
    All ! all !—my Saviour, wash them all ! "
And, ere the accents died away,
    The words were faltered forth again,

Till, with the feeble, fluttering breath,
    The youthful spirit passed away.

7

Oh! death in life—oh! life in death!
Night lost in Heaven's eternal day.

He sleeps! young soldier of the Cross;
    The fight is o'er—the victory won!
And, counting earthly treasure dross,
    Say, who will gird thy armor on?
For life is real—death is sure,
    And thou hast learned the triumph strain,
" Worthy the Lamb forevermore,
    Whose blood hath washed and made us
        clean."

*Tuesday, March* 17, 1868.

"*AND AFTER THE FIRE, A STILL SMALL
    VOICE.*"—1 KINGS xix. 13.

A SOUND of rushing wind has come
    Fearfully from afar,
Dark omen of the tempest's gloom,
    Of nature's dreaded war.
And low before the mighty blast
    Tall trees like reeds are bent;
Yet its terrific splendor passed—
    Nor was the mandate sent.

But hark! o'er all the trembling land
   Another sound is gone;
Earth, swayed by some resistless hand,
   Is shaken on her throne;
And rocks that mocked the tempest's power
   Are hurling through the air;
Yet passed the terror of that hour—
   Nor was the mandate there.

Once more, though still convulsed with fright,
   Nor yet the world is free;
For onward comes a blaze of light
   In grand sublimity.
And all the storm the shock may spare
   Is melted into flame,
But through the heated, melted air,
   Nor yet the mandate came.

Now all is hushed—the storm, the fire,
   The earthquake—all are past,
Nor mingled with one trace of ire
   Came that decree at last.
But borne along the silent air
   There breathes "a still small" tone—
*There* speaks the mighty One, and there
   He makes His mandate known.

## JACOB'S DREAM.

THE sunset's light had left the sky,
  The stars came glittering forth,
And evening in her quiet grace
  Fell gently o'er the earth.
He does not raise his eyes to meet
  Night in her glorious dress,
For other, sadder thoughts than these
  On his worn spirit press.

They are of home—a mother's love,
  A father's helpless age;
Himself an exile—never more
  To bless their pilgrimage.
'Twas this that quelled the heart of youth,
  For this the proud boy wept;
Till wearied, on the cold, damp earth
  He laid him down and slept.

Oh! hallowed was that lowly couch—
  No monarch's gorgeous bed
Had ever thrown so rich a light
  Around a sleeper's head.
For Heaven to his bewildered view
  Its glory now displays,
And angels pass in bright array
  Before the dreamer's gaze.

A voice is in his ears : it tells
   His fainting heart of peace.
Fear not !   I am thy Father's God ;
   Nor shall My mercies cease.
I will be with thee where thou art—
   On mountain-top or plain,
And bring thee to thy native land
   In might and power again.

He rose, and with the morning light
   Pursued his lonely way,
But not in darkness nor in dread
   Again his pathway lay ;
The cloud had passed from off his soul,
   Year after year swept on,
And found him in a hoary age
   God's blest—His chosen one.

---

## "*THE WORLD WAS YET YOUNG.*"

THE world was yet young—but its glory was
    past,
The foul breath of sin had laid loveliness waste ;
The world was yet young—but how changed since
    its birth,
For corruption and violence filled the whole earth.

And its daughters in beauty, its sons in their
    might,
Turned in scorn from the hand that would lead
    them aright,
Till the windows of Heaven were opened, and
    poured
From the fount of His vengeance the wrath of
    the Lord.


Oh! vain was the cry that went up in that hour,
From manhood struck down in the pride of his
    power;
While the maiden's bright tress swept o'er the
    dark wave,
And the infant's low wail reached no ear that
    could save.


Is mercy forgotten? Oh! God, from the land
Wilt Thou cut off forever the work of Thy hand?
Still, still leave a remnant, Thy name to declare,
To adore Thee in praise, and to worship in
    prayer.


And, lo! a frail barque on the water's broad
    breast
Is launched 'mid the billows, in safety to rest;
Till He who hath loosed it the deep shall en-
    chain,
And the myrtle and olive trees blossom again.

Now earth, with Thy children to grandeur re-
    stored,
Send up one glad shout to Thy covenant, Lord ;
And thus through all time shall His Church ride
    the wave,
For He who hath pledged it is mighty to save.

## LITTLE HENRY.

" GOOD-NIGHT—good-night, dear mother
    For I am sleepy now."
His mother took his little hand,
    And from his infant brow
She turned aside the silken curls,
    Then solemnly said :
" Henry—you have not said your prayers,
    And can you go to bed ?"

" No, dearest mother, no—
    Indeed, I did forget—
But I will pray with all my heart,
    And God will love me yet."
Then as he lisped his evening prayer
    Upon his mother's knee,
He kissed her cheek and whispered low,
    " God will take care of me."

When little Henry laid
    His weary head to rest,
He said that with the rising sun
    He would be up and dressed—
And running in the fresh green grass,
    Till near his favorite tree,
He'd stop to hear the little birds
    That sung so merrily.


Before the morning came
    A flush was on his cheek;
He could not raise his heavy eye,
    But once he tried to speak.
" Mother, I love to say my prayers,"
    Were all the words he said,
And ere another sun was set
    The lovely boy was dead.


O'er his early grave
    His sorrowing parents wept;
But they were not bitter tears, for there
    His body only slept.
His happy spirit was in heaven,
    And would you go there too ?
Morning and evening pray to God,
    And He'll take care of you.

## *HOLLYWOOD.*

"As it was at the creation—as it is now, and as it shall be at the end of the world."

B RIGHT was the morn—the sunshine fell
   In glory o'er the land ;
And nature, bursting into life,
   Struck with a trembling hand
A chord of praise from the dark leaves
   By gentle breezes stirred,
From the soft murmur of the brook—
   From the warble of the bird.

No cloud had ever dimmed the sky,
   Nor broke the ocean's rest,
But the daybeam slept in quietness
   On the mighty monarch's breast ;
No tone of sorrow e'er had lent
   Its wailing to the air ;
A holy peace was on the Earth—
   Sin had not entered there.

What wert thou then ? A little spot
   Decked in its robe of green ;
Beside the haughty mountain tops
   Thy beauty all unseen ;
But now thou art our treasure-place,
   A bow is o'er thee spread,
Set in the cloud of sorrowing hearts,
   To bind them to their dead.

We bring our beautiful to thee ;
  The mother, at whose breast
An infant flower had fallen asleep,
  Has laid it here to rest ;
To thee we bring our aged ones,—
  Our statesmen in their pride,—
And those, alas ! who in the flush
  Of youth and hope have died.

Here sheltered by embattled walls,
  Lulled by the water's flow,
Walls, iron-tongued, undying fame
  In history to know,
Thousands of Southern soldiers rest,
  Heroes of song and story ;
Who wove, in death for Freedom's life,
  The mantle of their glory.

Oh ! hushed and sacred be the spot,
  Where oft at twilight grey,
The stricken mourner bends her steps
  To weep her grief away ;
Where oft the strong man's spirit bows
  O'er joys forever fled ;
And stranger tears bedew the sod
  That marks the unknown dead.

But hark ! whence comes that thrilling sound,
  That pealing trumpet blast ?

And see th' Archangel high in air
  His dazzling splendors cast.
At that dread summons myriads burst
  Their chains beneath the sod;
And thou once more left tenantless—
  They stand before their God.

---

## A LETTER.

THIRTY-FIVE years—thirty-five years !
  Lights and shadows—smiles and tears !
Dark and bright colors skilfully wrought,
Blending in harmony, action, and thought.
Now to completion the pattern nears—
Two lives in one, for all these years.

Little I thought as I stood at your side
Young and gay-hearted, a happy bride,
All the deep import of words that fell
Solemnly, tenderly—yet it was well
Fearless and trusting to go to my home,
There to be sheltered these years to come.

Youth, with its upspringing hope and faith,
Carved out triumphs that mock at death;
Summer, perfecting them, passed away,
Bearing the burden and heat of the day;

Autumn is waning, and now we come
Joyful to garner our harvest home.

Time must leave footprints in thirty-five years;
Joys spring alternate with sadness and tears.
But "goodness and mercy" forsaking us never,
Ourselves and our children—Lord, keep us for-
    ever,
And while to the sunset the dial still nears,
May Love mark the shadows for all coming years.

*35th Anniversary of Wedding-day.*

V. M. INSTITUTE, *June* 9, 1870.

———

The "sunset" of life in its sadness has come;
For the shadows of death now rest on our home;
But Faith lifts the veil that conceals from our
    eyes
The peace of the loved one at rest in the skies;
And thanks be to God, who hath knit us together,
"Two lives in one" still united *forever*.

*May* 18, 1884.